For Silvia, June & Aunty I,
my Birmingham buddies
— with BIG hugs —
S.P-H.

With a great big thank-you hug
to the unstoppable Hannah Whitty
A.B.

BLOOMSBURY CHILDREN'S BOOKS
Bloomsbury Publishing Plc
50 Bedford Square, London, WC1B 3DP, UK
29 Earlsfort Terrace, Dublin 2, Ireland

BLOOMSBURY, BLOOMSBURY CHILDREN'S BOOKS and the Diana logo are trademarks of Bloomsbury Publishing Plc
First published in Great Britain 2023

Text copyright © Smriti Prasadam-Halls, 2023
Illustrations copyright © Alison Brown, 2023

Smriti Prasadam-Halls and Alison Brown have asserted their rights under the Copyright, Designs and Patents Act, 1988,
to be identified as the Author and Illustrator of this work

A catalogue record for this book is available from the British Library

ISBN: 978 1 5266 3574 7 (HB)   978 1 5266 3575 4 (PB)   978 1 5266 3565 5 (eBook)

2 4 6 8 10 9 7 5 3 1

Printed and bound in Italy by L.E.G.O. S.P.A

MIX
Paper | Supporting
responsible forestry
FSC
www.fsc.org
FSC® C023419

All papers used by Bloomsbury Publishing Plc are natural, recyclable products from wood grown in well managed forests.
The manufacturing processes conform to the environmental regulations of the country of origin

To find out more about our authors and books visit www.bloomsbury.com
and sign up for our newsletters

The VERY BEST HUG

Smriti Halls   Alison Brown

BLOOMSBURY
CHILDREN'S BOOKS
LONDON OXFORD NEW YORK NEW DELHI SYDNEY

Have you ever wondered who gives the BEST hug?

The kind that's warm and cosy and snug?

Extra squeezy, but never too tight,

The kind that fits you completely right?

Well, let's find out.

I wonder,

have you tried . . .

A Bear Hug?

Or a
Koala Cuddle?

How about . . .

a Seahorse
Smooch?

Or a
Hippo Huddle?

Not **quite** sure about those?

Ah, you think the bubbles

might get up your nose?

And hippos **are** quite heavy

I suppose . . .

Well then, how about . . . .

A Kangaroo Kiss?

Or a Walrus Wiggle?

A Penguin Peck?

Or a Porcupine Prickle?

I SEE . . .

You're right, there's not
much room in that pouch.

And those beaks and spikes
are quite an OUCH!

(And that walrus does look a bit of a grouch.)

But no problem, look . . .

Narwhals like to **nuzzle**,

nightingales love to **nestle**,

raccoons like to **wriggle,**

and **rhinos** love to . . . .

. . . WRESTLE!

Whoops! Fair enough.
You might not be quite ready to rumble
in THIS rambunctious rough and tumble!
But how about . . .

A
Skunk Squeeze?

Or a
Squirrel Snuggle?

A Cobra
Clinch?

Or a Hedgehog
Huggle?

And if you're **brave** and you think you dare,
there are hugs to be had just over there . . .

You could step into
that furry-purry lair for . . .

A Lion Squish! Or a Leopard Squash!

A Monkey Mash!

Or a Meerkat Mosh!

Oh, WHAT an amazing

But, oh dear – you don't think the best hug
is ANY of these?

(Well, to be honest, you're really
quite hard to please . . .)

Unless . . .

Hold on a minute!

Who gives the best hugs?
You've got it!
You've guessed!

It's the ones at home, who **love** you the best!

Extra squeezy, but never too tight,
the kind that fit you completely right.
Warm and cosy and cuddly and snug –
Well done! You've found . . .

...the VERY best hug!